# armed
## to the teeth
## with LIPSTICK

# armed to the teeth with LIPSTICK

## blag DAHLIA marc RUDE

**GREEDY** P.O. BOX 170481
SAN FRANCISCO CA
9 4 1 1 7

"Armed to the Teeth with Lipstick"
©1989 Greedy
Words © Blag Dahlia
Art © Marc Rude

First Printing 1998
ISBN 0-9664432-0-9

Cover design by Marc Rude
Book design by Gary Hustwit

All rights reserved. No part of this book may be
reproduced or transmitted in any form or by any means,
electronic or mechanical, including photocopying, recording,
or any information storage and retrieval system, without
permission in writing from the copyright holder.

This planet Earth has reached the point
of no return.

Let's put them weenies on a stick
and watch it burn.

- Anonymous

# 1.
# MORNING HORROR

Saturday morning. I rose from a night of chemical revelry and cursed the day I was born. Doolan's the name, the heat gone cold loco and paying in spades. Jungle beat — Mars, the Red Planet, a sleeping giant with one foot on the gas pedal and one on Lovers Leap.

They said you couldn't keep it down once I'd seen some action and I guess 'they' were right. In twelve long years with the Korps I'd tasted enough senseless carnality for a lifetime, and truth be told I couldn't tell the black hats from the white anymore. In my business that meant trouble.

Cut to a park bench sunrise. I'm pissed to be taken away from my dreaming, cold in the dry heaving sunlight. A breath of fake fur and lipstick eased up from the gutter. Eyeballs red as a streetwalker's labia flashed on the daytime world and thought —

"Satan's are we, Satan's am I."

See, Mars has a dark side. I'd found it once the old lady got real, real gone for a change. Human she was, all too human, and I was from this world so you can bet we made quite an eyeload promenading down the boulevard of broken genes. It didn't pay to dwell there, though.

Unnameable dread dogged each step as I pondered the futility of the good fight and the high cost of crystal methedrine on a world gone kerplunk. Then, without a warning, the sky lit up napalm yellow and all thoughts were in vain.

    Urban terror was heavy this season. Some sorehead with an axe to grind must have laced the pavement with plastic explosives. The blast sent me reeling — shaken, but none the worse for heavy shrapnel. Another day, another delirium.

    See, we imported weapons and tactics and women from your world, that's true, but on Mars we'd just about cornered the market on survival of the fittest. The rabid pioneers who'd settled this orb had thrived and mutated, carving out a space age Sodom that burned while the Korps kept an uneasy peace. And We The People just kept shooting and reproducing with a vengeance.

    That's why I was an X-cop, the best kind. Standard issue with the license to kill came a dozen splinter grenades and a modified Luger for nostalgia's sake. When I needed more I just upped the arsenal, and my personal favorite was a Fly-Rite Yo-Yo cast in osmium. This yo-yo was a motherfukker.

    Now usually a sneak attack would find me plotting my own messy ending and eventual sainthood, but this time paranoia gripped me hard, nads first. I started to shake and convulse, teeth gnashing tongue, nose drooling a thick red foam. When Vesuvius erupted across my cranium I started firing, busting off rounds in a tweek raging fit.

    Hollow points flew as empty eyes peered from broken windows. I heard a dead baby cry. In the Korps we're trained to believe that violence is golden, but I couldn't help thinking regret is a whore with wings.

Finally, a figure emerged in a Red Cross nurse's uniform and white stockings, the severe bun on her head held in place by a hari-kari dagger. It was my secretary, Miss Vaggner. She was mean, she was vicious, but there was something about her I liked. Somehow she kept my crank-addled brain from oozing out the hole in my noggin.

"Any calls for me?"

"One, from Korps EQ. I told them you were drinking and couldn't be disturbed."

"Swell."

# 2.
# A FRENZIED TRIBUTE TO THE VOID

"Herr Doolan, I have taken the liberty of purging your files of certain unpleasant materials. The Korps has informed me that my services are required elsewhere, but if you need further assistance just dial 999 on any touchtone phone..."

By now I'd stopped wondering why my secretary always left the building as soon as I'd returned, and as the door slammed shut behind her I glanced at my day bed, its hospital corners so sharp they could circumsize. She worked hard for the money, and work liberates us all. It also put grub on the table, something I'd been hurting for.

See, I was classified freelance, with a wink and a nod from the boys at the Virtual Vice Korps. When it came down to necessary force, the VVK was untouchable, no rodents in the apple pie, but everybody in the know knew that my days in the Korps were numbered.

Imagine a kind of Salivation Army, keeping this world free from recreational sex and too loose expressionism. The guys who snuffed Stravinsky and replaced him with a bust of Lawrence Welk, sans the champagne, and I'd gone from top of the class to bottom of the barrel when I'd discovered just how good a bad time can be.

Mars was a hell of a spot, with too many channels

and nothing but filth in the dragnet. That left me home most nights, drunk and tweeking the dials that spun in my watery melon.

I didn't miss the action, though. Empty days were filled with visions of the Earth, of my mother's land. That world was big and wide and green; and populated by harlots fully seven feet tall. It was said you could cut lines of gak on their flanks and douche them with Dom Perignon, then go home and watch the whole sick spectacle on daytime TV.

Something like that.

Anyway, it was all just a leadpipe dream. Martian NASA was strictly from hunger, so like it or else I was stuck here, watching the minutes pass like mud through an hourglass.

A dusty 45 skidded across my ancient Victrola. I fixed a highball and a hot-shot in a frenzied tribute to the void. Later, an angry red light called the teleview awakened me.

# 3.
# EMOTIONAL MANSLAUGHTER

The call was from my ball and chain, a piece of work called the Equalizer. First in command and last to scream uncle, the EQ had taken so many blows for the empire they'd just done away with his physical form and transistorized him instead.

The official line was that he'd given up his body in the name of Korps security, but we'd come up through the ranks together and I'd seen him go Stalin, then solid state. A certain fatal femme had thrown him the gasface and he'd wound up crucified on an ugly stick. There were only a handful of us left who knew him when, and it wasn't very pretty for us either.

"Doolan, you drunken broom, stand at attention when I buzz you."

"I'm working on a decent buzz right now."

"My daughter Suzi has been truant from school all week, and she didn't come home last night. I want her found immediately and returned to me."

No surprises there. Ever since little Suzy-Q got out of kneepants everything that she did or didn't do rated as a minor apocalypse with the old man. Coming up with that kind of baggage and no female around to smooth out the wet spots...well, let's say I felt for her.

At the same time, I was in need of some gainful employment, and the EQ knew that old dependable, expendable Doolan could be counted on to dummy up in a family crisis.

"Where does she hang and who is she with?"

On his big, ugly screen I saw a picture of the Old Fairgrounds and mug shots of a few surly delinquents. Then Suzy's face appeared in a halo of yearning and Clearasil, and for a second there I almost lost my grip.

See, in the Korps we don't always go by the book. Sometimes, it's got to be statutory.

"Why don't you give the kid a break, maybe the collarbone?"

"There'll be no more nonsense from her. This time she'll go straight to Rebellion Control."

Rebellion Control was a juvenile snakepit, wielding the cleaver on wards of the state. High spirited Jeckyls checked in, but half the time it was narco happy Hydes who checked out. And when the inmates got wind of who her father was, she'd be drawn, quartered, and left for puppy chow.

"That's emotional manslaughter, they'll depersonalize the damn kid!"

"Now you're an expert on child rearing as well as drug addiction, Doolan? If I see fit she'll haunt a bloody nunnery."

There was no use arguing the point, so I accessed the spirit of Tina Peel and started thinking tactically. When I hear the word female I reach for my Luger. Young hearts bleed lead, and glycerine tears are the least of my worries.

"This gang that she's running with is posing as a musical outfit called Lucifers Crank; but be forewarned — they are armed and extremely talentless."

"Happy trails to you too, Chief," I said to an empty screen.

# 4.
# A THERMOS FULL OF DAQUIRIS

The Old Fairgrounds were ripe with stickball and Gatorade and my mind wandered back to the Gidgets of yore. Some said life was easier then, I guess meaning the women were. More often than not, with the gentle persuasion of a thermos full of daquiris, me and the crew would wind up knee deep in huevos. But, that was then, and the good old days were dead and gone.

It was still life here though, fairly teeming with nubiles and punks, and though it did my black heart good to see some urban resuscitation, I had the sinking feeling that my honeymoon was over and I'd missed the rerun too.

It was then that I spotted the Equalizer's daughter, Suzy-Q, lounging among the jet flotsam of a new generation. She was pale, freckled, and if she went topless, well you couldn't tell it by me. I guess she was growing up though, judging by the pout heavy posture she assumed upon sighting yours truly.

It seemed like a shame to put her away, but I was three lines from stable as it was and all I really wanted was a stranger's bed and a window to jump out of. I also knew that one more slider meant wipe-out. I gritted my teeth and approached.

"Hey Suzy, long time no see."

She wasn't surprised to see me, but thrilled

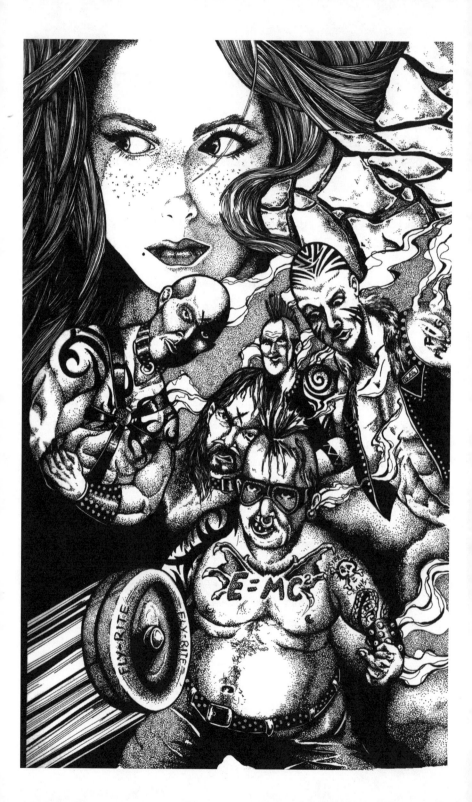

wouldn't be quite accurate either. I figured she'd let some sparks fly and she didn't disappoint.

"Daddy told me they donated your liver to science and it came back postage due."

Before I could muster a reply, a young hardtail, one notch above Neanderthal, stepped to the fore flanked by four bubble-head henchmen. His hair was every color of the blessed rainbow and on his scabby chest was a tattoo of $E=mc^2$, the transmartian symbol for too much, too soon. He opened his hole and you just knew that toastmaster wasn't his bag.

"Dry up gumshoe, before I put my foot in your ass and kick your damn head in."

Now, I've been trained to believe that timing is everything. I took a good look at the terrain, pulled out the old Fly-Rite and gave it a couple of experimental twirls. Then I let Mr. Congenial have it right between the eyes. With my boot firmly in his backside, and the razor wire around his throat, I told his buddies one false move and he was history.

The blood poured green off his neck and onto my hands. It felt good. As he gasped toward unconsciousness I even found myself enjoying his company for the first time since we'd met. The feeling didn't seem to be mutual though, so before he made pals with the Reaper I put on my bad doggie voice and ordered Suzy to come home with me. And then something wicked happened.

The punks and their women were bathed in a weird eerie light. Then they rose up off the ground ever so slightly and vanished in a puff of formaldehyde.

It was one of those moments when you feel the car that is your life careen into a brick wall in gruesome slow motion and before you hit, you already know it's over. I lit up a Lucky and rolled my eyes to the heavens. Something told me I should have been aiming a little further south.

# 5.
# AN ASSHOLE WHEN I DRINK

"Mickey, gimme three fingers of Lingonberry Schnapps, a Tequila Simpson, and eight buckwheat pancakes."

I added another glassful to the pool of vomit that all but obscured a basket of stale pretzels gathering moss in front of the only barkeep in town who'd still serve me even after my intestines had cut me off.

"Why don't you just go home, Doolan?"

"Why don't you stuff a cork in it, mushmouth?"

"Rayguns and teenagers and mass hallucinations... go sleep it off for Christ sakes!"

That tore it. I'd seen this old fukk hoist a Tizer on a dehydrated boy-scout, now he wanted me to cool it? I busted a fifth on the bar and brandished it.

"I tell you they disappeared, motherfukker, prepare to die!"

Did I forget to mention that I'm an asshole when I drink? And I always drink alone. With malice pulling my heartstrings and the jagged bottle cocked behind my back, I suddenly felt the ominous sting of VVK regulation handcuffs.

"Field Martian Lucifer Doolan?"

With a quickness the bar was alive with MPs who knew me by reputation, and they weren't taking any chances. Like the Red Army storming a blue heaven they came, and once again my wanting face met another man's ceiling.

"Sir, you'll have to come with us."

"Buy me a drink and I'll come on anybody."

They dragged me kicking and screaming to the door.

# 6.
# SPIRALLING TOWARD THE FLOOR

"This court will come to order."

"You clowns couldn't come in a Mexican barnyard," I screamed, getting a cold slap in the face for my trouble.

When I went to return it the effort sent me spiralling toward the floor. Slowly I began to put it all together. The straight-jacket, the fancy office, the EQ decked out on his video monitor in a dapper old world judge's robe and wig.

Court Martial! The last hurrah before your bloody corpus adorns the pavement. Justice is blind on my planet. It also has a bad case of dysentery.

"Field Martian Lucifer Doolan, you are charged with the crime of negligence in the abduction of my daughter. How do you plead?"

Now, I can plead with the best of 'em. Just ask the ex-Mrs. Doolan. I can plead ignorance, insanity or demonic possession and still not be scratching the surface. That wasn't going to cut it this time. The powers that be were working on the railroad and I was modeling pancake suits. Meanwhile, the figure to my right slapped me hard again. He was my attorney.

"Do you deny that you were drunk and deluded on duty? That you were derelict in defense of my daughter?"

It was starting to look like they'd amputated my leg to stand on, but I stated my case once again. A tale that boiled down to a resounding thud on the plausibility meter.

"There's thin air between your ears, Doolan. How do you make seven teenagers disappear?"

I told him if I knew that I'd be Pope by now, but no one heard me in the confusion. A messenger had come in and plugged into the Equalizer's command center, (the closest the EQ could come to carnal knowledge) and once he'd gotten the binomial word the room got very quiet. Then he dropped a neutron bombshell, and when it was over I'd wish it hadn't left me standing.

Apparently, the boys in the little white suits had been working overtime on a new pop-gun. Nothing novel in that. As long as I could remember those eggheads had been promising an end to armed conflict through better weapons. Like you'd sheath a bigger willy to make shade for the ant-eaters. This time though, they hit it big.

Enter the Time/Space Warp. A little number that could break down matter, transport and reassemble it fast as a conjugal visit. This explained those pasty teens abrupt departure. What it didn't explain was anything else.

A close-up of the Warp appeared where the EQ's face had been, then slowly it began to morph into a cheesecake shot of a homicidal pin-up girl. The Equalizer's disembodied voice came booming from every speaker.

"Last week the plans for, and a prototype of, the Time/Space Warp were stolen from Korps EQ. The top secret nature of the project made it difficult to trace the perpetrators, but it is believed to be the work of..."

My heart sank, my blood boiled and my rod stood bolt upright. That face, those menacing eyes, those sulphurous lips, but... she was dead! I knew she was dead.

The picture flicked off the screen, replaced by the EQ's hideous maw. He didn't have to, but he said it. Said the name I thought I'd buried forever.

"...Natasha Romilar and her twisted assistant Faust."

# 7.
# LETHAL DRAG

In a penthouse apartment overlooking Scarlet Square, a woman shaped like a halfback in lethal drag surveyed the city below. There was something hard in her beauty, sugar on a pneumatic drill. She moved in an orbit heavy with gravity, mixing this potion with that, destination zero.

The face, white as death, glowed by the light of a bunsen burner in the only chemical research laboratory in creation with an ocelot color scheme and Persian houri candles. In her languorous Balkan accent she said —

"Fix me another speedball, won't you, darling?"

Faust, her doting lab-rat, prepared two big bangs after selecting from a batch of dirty needles on the coffee table.

"And go easy on the cocaine, I'm in no mood for idle conversation."

Not to be cruel, but Faust was an odd looking creature. Short, yes; but no midget, no cute little micro-sapien. He was a dwarf. Deformed and proud, with a head too large for his legs and too small for his appetite. He couldn't speak as clearly as he could think, or make love like they did in the movies. He could scrap though, like a savage.

"This has been quite an afternoon, Faust. Not

only have we confirmed the viability of the Time/Space Warp, we've also served notice that the Korps is powerless to stop us."

Natasha was confident, but Faust had spent ten years in solitary confinement after our last get together, and he knew it was too soon for champagne wishes and caviar dreams.

"The Korps...wormy, rotten...Doolan...parched throat...bleeding heart..."

Her eyes said — "I'll make him sorry," as they bumped rigs and shot the stars a toast to never.

# 8.
# OH! DEM GOLDEN ARCHES

Far from anywhere like heaven, seven Martian youths appeared where before there was only dust and sagebrush. They looked from one to another, then toward the sky, a sky as lonely and unfamiliar as an albino whore. Lifetimes spent in front of the shortwave watching pirate broadcasts of *The Jetsons* and *Leave it to Beaver* hadn't been wasted, though. When one of them noticed golden arches far away in the distance, they knew where fate had placed them. Mother Earth — the original rock 'n' roll planet.

"This is fukking great," said Gizmo.

Gizmo was a roadie. Six-foot five, two-hundred thirty pounds and smart as a bag of hammers. He'd just been hired that week by Buckley, the tour manager, and he needed the job, but he couldn't help feeling there was something weird about this scene. These dudes did a lot of crimes and stuff, but they never seemed to play any music.

There was Atom on guitar, Eddie on bass and Trash on drums, that much he knew, but what they sounded like was anybody's guess. They had to be pretty good, though. They had two fine Betties with them and an Earth tour, didn't they?

After the initial confusion had worn off, everybody started jawing at once. Finally, they agreed that Earth was the place to be, especially since they didn't have any choice. And if British people could make records here, they might as well let Martians try it, too.

Trash spotted headlights down the road coming toward them. A huge cloud of dust kicked up on either side of the semi as it came into view, giving it an air of spiritual importance. The men of Lucifers Crank waved frantically, and as it ground to a halt they could see that the side of the truck was vast and painted with stars and spheres in ridiculous neon shades.

The door opened and a bearded throwback drawled —

"Greetings weary desert folk."

They got in anyway. A hatch in the cab opened out into the hull of the truck where the decor was a kind of mondo Graceland with a healthy dose of new age sham shamanism. Fully equipped as a rehearsal space with its own generator, the main attraction for the Martians was the fully stocked wet bar and vintage KISS pinball machine.

"Are you guys in a rock 'n' roll band?" asked Buckley, eyeing an original Kozik with darts in it. There was an uncomfortable pause as the pretensions grew thicker.

"We prefer the term Audio/Visceral Engineers."

A few miles outside of Flagstaff, Eddie's on again/off again girl started feeling her oats while she got in a bag. Her name was Angel and it fit like a

jimmy hat on a two-year-old. Peroxide and lipstick and wide open spaces dominated her skullwork, not that you'd notice with the rest of her present and very well accounted for.

As the night wore on, Angel's inhibitions all but disappeared in a web of philosophical double-talk and pharmaceuticals. By the time the hippie driver had pulled over to meditate by the light of the lunar equinox, she was drooling like Pavlov's dog. Even Suzy-Q, not quite old enough to care, was smitten. They had never met a real band before, not one from Earth anyway.

And the boys from The Crank could see the writing on the outhouse wall. With a moon like cleavage in the sky they hijacked the semi, leaving their unfortunate hosts on the desert floor in the lotus position, dilated eyes lolling heavenward, contemplating the age old mystery of dehydration.

Then, like wolves in an alcoholic hen house, they hit the bar hard. Angel and Suzy never looked backwards.

# 9.
# SIAMESE TWIN PROSTITUTES

The EQ went blank as a critic's cranium, but the image still haunted me. So, Natasha was in on this bottle of furry capers, too? If I wasn't presumed guilty before setting foot in this kangaroo court, I didn't have a harlot's prayer now.

Natasha Romilar. SheWhoCanNotBeNamed. The sight of my (who was I kidding, everybody's) long lost concubine almost made me forget where I was and who I was going to.

"Doolan, I have always been the first to leap to your defense in these matters. When you appeared at the annual Korps Masquerade Ball with a syringe poking out of your arm, did I not claim that you were dressed as a pincushion? And when you arranged conjugal visits with Ethyl and Ella, the Siamese twin prostitutes, did I not turn a blind eye to your... peccadilloes?"

"That was the research opportunity of a lifetime."

"This outrage is inexcusable, intolerable...in short, Doolan, the theft of the Time/Space Warp puts the Korps and the citizens of Mars in great peril..."

At that my trusty mouthpiece and two MPs with black hoods and lead-lined suits wheeled in a contraption that looked like a cannon with a telefloral

# SIAMESE·TWIN prostitutes

lens on it. They say that at times like this your whole life passes before your eyes like oil on velvet, but all I could see was the reckless leer and bedroom hips of my arch-obler, Natasha.

"...this prototype, untested as of today, will have you as the object of its maiden voyage."

So that was that. Mortality is a pleasure trip, but exile? I'd been just about everywhere that I wanted to go and a few places I didn't, so I did what we all do when confronted by the inevitable. I kicked and screamed and stamped my little feet.

"Tell me, Oh Great One — in the depths of your android, cock tease, TV mediocrity, did you ever stop to think where this game is headed and what it is you really want from me? Haven't I walked the tightrope in your little flea circus long enough to warrant some answers? I've been dead to the world for so long that I'm puking up brimstone. I don't eat, I don't sleep, and I don't do windows..."

These outbursts of mine can be scary. One minute I'm fine, and the next I'm a raving lunatic. They say speed kills, I guess crank is Murder One. What did it matter anyway; death, where is thy stink?

"Doolan, I pity the fool."

And with that he was gone.

See, my affection for the little blue ball by Venus was an open secret in the Korps. Because my mother was an Earthling wench I'd always had to work twice as hard for half as much, but not knowing math I'd never really noticed. Now it looked like I was bound for the terra-dome, like it or else.

I saw the same eerie glow as that day in the park and I knew soon I'd be nothing but gnarly nougat streaking through the Milky Way. I just hoped for once I was wrapped up tightly.

## 10.
## EVERYONE'S A WINNER

The bright lights hit my eyes like a fist. I knew where I was, I guess I'd always known. There are no secret destinations, no cruel twists of fate. My ancestors were given to extra-terrestrial dalliance, which explained the dual citizenship of my respiratory system and my love of a good time. What it didn't explain was — what now?

The US of A in my mind's eye was a kaleidoscope of scratchy 45s and movie magazines, the realm of Li'l Orphan OJ and the Possee Comatosis. Nothing mama done told me between gulps of grain liquor could have prepared me for the decaying giant known as Times Square, or the senseless corruption that oozed from every pore of its volcanic multitude.

"Alright, step up, everyone's a winner, everybody wins and nobody loses."

It sounded like Pro Wrestling to me, but what the hell? I moved to a spot near the front where a little rat in designer sweats and a doo-rag was holding court. His pin prick eyes alighted on me.

"Sir, you seem like a smart man, a wise man, maybe even a family man..."

"Get to the point."

"I've got three cards in front of me, as you can

see. Two are black and one is red. Pick the red one and you're a winner, do you have five dollars, sir? Remember, everyone's a winner."

I checked the pockets of my rumpled suit pants. Sure enough, they'd slipped me some loot before the blackout. It was easy come, easy action.

"I got five on it."

"Show me the five and you're a winner, sir. Which card is it?"

A crowd had formed around us and I smelled con as thick as the ozone. I'd seen some jokers guess the red, but they were obvious set-ups. Still, you can't win for losing. I pointed to a card.

"Sorry, sir, but that was close, look again because it happens very fast. Where's the red card now? Five dollars."

Mesmerized, I looked at his cold hands moving across the top of that orange crate. I thought about hands across the water. Then hands across the cosmos and then hands across this bastard's throat if I came up short again. I was sure I had hit it this time.

"Wrong again, sir, but put up ten and you get twenty back, no one leaves a loser. Sir, you strike me as an intelligent man."

Did I mention that I hate to lose?

"You also strike me as an honest man, sir."

"I just might strike you period, pal," I said, watching the black card come up yet again.

"Put up fifty, you're a guaranteed winner."

"Tell you what," I said, pulling out my Luger and pointing it straight at his heart, "I'll trade ya."

The dealer ran fast, leaving the cash and a stain where his stool used to be. I guess there's a sucker born every minute. I bought a bag of yellow powder off a dead end kid and pulled up a gutter seat. Now that amateur hour was over, I had to face the cold hard lavatory floor.

Somehow, find Suzy. Not for the EQ or the Korps, not even for her sake, but for mine. I figured my best bet would be to access New York's Finest for strategic advice, back up, and maybe a boysenberry danish. I also knew that stories of interstellar abduction might just win me a spot on the Bellvue Express, but I figured I could use the practice weaving baskets.

I snorted a big line of gak, cursing my weakness of spirit and the high cost of pleasure on planet Earth.

# 11.
# POWDER KEG HELL-HOLE

Natasha and Faust landed farther uptown than tourists are usually encouraged to go and, in all their years of searching, they'd never seen such glorious decay. Rotting brownstones rose and fell under a terminal grey sky. Together, they drank in the dope, death and despair of the teeming millions yearning to breathe free airplane glue in a plastic bag on a fire escape. What better place than this to launch their masturbatory plans?

They spotted three young girls jumping rope, double-dutch in the street. Natasha, maternal as a black widow spider, and Faust, the malevolent smurf, did nothing to put them at their ease.

"Where did you come from?" asked one little girl, too young to be afraid.

"We're from an inner space, dear. Tell me, do you live out here on the boulevard?"

The little one pointed toward a dilapidated four-story walk-up off in the distance.

"Your parents, they have abandoned you to a life of petty crime and stultifying boredom. When they do grace you with their presence, they're too busy fornicating with the television on to know that you even exist, isn't that right?"

The rope stopped turning and the girls became nervously quiet. Then one of them burst into tears and the three of them ran off sobbing down the street. Natasha turned on her heel like MacArthur in a tiki lounge.

"Children, I shall return."

As twilight fell, the stares that followed the pair of them got uglier. A woman like Natasha commands attention anywhere, but here she was a gyrating powder-keg. Behind them they felt eyes boring holes in their backs, legs catching up to them. Finally, five teenage hoods with their own movable soundtrack pulled the inevitable.

First, there was the name calling and intimidation and, when his patience had worn thin, there was Faust. On Mars a man's size isn't important. Limbs are built for violent disruption, but attitude won battles and Faust had a motherlode.

The little man strangled one of the juvenile jokers until he turned blue, eyes bulging out like a slaughtered bass. The comrade who came to his aid with a broken malt liquor bottle got it returned the hard way, right through his colon.

Natasha ripped off her shirt and shot from the areolas a nerve gas designed to peel the skin off of your throat. (That little trick was a souvenir of the time that she mainlined a silo full of World War I surplus goods and washed it down with a plutonium chaser.) Thirty seconds later the melée was history.

To put it mildly, the street thugs got a Martian jolt and they never came back for seconds.

The she-wolf and her runt surveyed the damage that fit in so well with the sprawl of the sick, naked city. Natasha's face was pensive, her brows cutting a wide furrow on her smooth white forehead, a look that usually meant disaster of the pay-me-now-or-pay-me-later variety. Then a smile crept over her blood red lips.

"What perfectly tacky little jogging outfits. Can't these gangsters wear something a bit...earthier? And this music..."

With that she set off a depth charge under the oversized boom-box that sent it spiraling into orbit, sprinkling plastic shrapnel everywhere and replacing the hard driving funk that had been the brawls' theme with an eerie, celestial silence.

"It's enough to wake the dead," she mused, and they walked on contented.

# 12.
# ENOUGH RUTHLESS OBSCENITY

Walking up the dung brown staircase of Precinct 5-0 was almost like coming home. Pigs the universe over share a love of senseless violence and no taste in interior decorating. Shapeless meter maids, their assets like the back of a Greyhound bus ambled by on their way to traffic court. A black kid flanked by two white uniforms got bounced along the corridor. Like a john caught red-handed I wondered why I came in the first place.

My mind drifted to the days of wayback, when Mars was a wide open planet and The People really needed us. Rescuing fresh faced innocents from nuclear gang rape, keeping the press free of bomb planting goons...I even helped an old lady cross a minefield once.

Then she came along. Six feet of sub-atomic gash on spiked heels. That's when the nightmares started and the reel and rock and the methedrine I.V.'s. But she never got my soul, and when push came to shove I pulled the plug like a good little soldier. Only bad dreams don't die. They multiply like rats. And I'd been running so long I wasn't getting anywhere fast.

I had to find Suzy, and not for my soul, damned as I was. No, just for the fukk of it. And if these earthling flatfoots could help me, so help me, I'd use them.

I came to a door that said 'VICE' and opened it wide. Caught in the heat of conversation these rookies didn't even notice me. I heard the tail end of a bad joke and the roar of nasty laughter.

"Alright you clowns, enough ruthless obscenity. How goes the homo hunting?"

This loaded query was posed by a crew-cut mastodon of a man, three-hundred pounds if he was an ounce, with a dull glint in his eye that said — touch me, I'm sick.

A beat cop with stubble peeking out from under pancake makeup finished daubing at his lips with 'Queen Crimson #5' and said in a guttural Brooklynese —

"Just peachy, Lieutenant. This little Halston number you picked up for me catches more queers than a douche full of vaseline."

Now I've worked undercover, even under the influence, but these nuts were so caught up with fruit baiting they still hadn't noticed me. I wondered how the guy in the mini-skirt pulled any johns at all with a badge pinned to his blouse and a big yellow happy-face sticker that read — 'Hi! my name is Sgt. X.' He looked up at his partner.

"I just wish I could get some help from the Sarge here. Every time I need him he's in the latrine."

A squinky little termite in white labwear looked up from a reeking microscope, pure venom on his face.

"How many times must I tell you, idiot, I'm collecting samples!"

The Lieutenant and Sgt. X snickered like they knew what was coming next, but the funky doctor just kept yakking onward.

"The Scatology department is grossly understaffed and underappreciated. I'm about ready to wash my hands of the whole operation. And where is that lab assistant I was promised? Must I labor alone like Sisyphus forever?"

"Hey, you said I was in charge of Sisyphus this week, and gonorrhea too, Lieutenant."

I'd heard just about enough of this internal combustion, so I entered stage left.

"Simmer down ya milky meat-toasts. I'm Doolan — VVK."

# 13.
# JESUS ON PROM NIGHT

They eyed me like a rabbit in a snake pit for about three New York seconds. Then the guy in the labcoat rushed up and whispered in my ear —

"I'm Sgt. Saltpeter. You must be my new lab assistant, you seem the scatological sort. Tell me, are you experienced in the gentle art of collecting stools from the homeless and criminal element?"

He whipped a smeared pamphlet from his pocket and shoved it under my nose.

"This is my magnum opus, *Feces as Friend*."

Now I'm not what you'd call squeamish, but I do have my limitations. And when it comes to scatology, I figure let 'em eat urinal cake.

"Can the potty talk, dicknose. The name's Doolan, hard and raw in regard to the law. I'd like to register an intergalactic missing harlot report."

Saltpeter's jaw went slack and he slumped back to his cubby hole looking dejected. I guess he wasn't very tough shit after all. I turned to the Lieutenant and his transvestite flunky.

"I'm looking for a little cream puff named Suzy-Q. She disappeared a couple of light years ago and I'm hot on her trail."

No response. Just a pair of vacant eyes with skulls to match.

"I'm a cosmic greaser pig," I said, clutching at crazy straws, "maybe the last."

I pulled out my badge, the old VVK branded on a shiny brass pentagram. It didn't mean much on the red planet, and from the empty stares I was getting here it didn't look like it meant dookie in this neck of the woods either.

"You know anything about Vice, pal?"

Lt. Grizzle looked like a teddy bear with a thyroid problem, hair cropped close and folds of greasy flesh spilling out of a stained white t-shirt. When he opened his yap I could see the Black Hole of Calcutta. I figured an explanation was in order, but all of a sudden I felt the same epileptic rush I'd had that day when I blitzkreiged my office. Without consulting my grey matter my mouth tossed out this little gem —

"On Mars we've got Jesus in our corner on Prom Night. He's this real gone Tom Jones-type character who does shit like fukking two aryan girls simultaneously, and blindfolding them so they won't know they're sisters. But, in the end, they like it anyway, and one grows up rich and the other's good looking."

I could tell by their dazed expressions that I was losing them. Hell, I was losing myself. The speed down here was more potent than I realized. I gamely clamored on.

"Can't you true douche-bags savvy? I shit jelly beans and fukk a blue streak, and when I turn out the lights at night I hear the *Third Man Theme* like through a vibrating egg prism. I know it's kinda septica/spiritual and all, but where I come from a man's crank has to be in five-wheel drive or his Old Lady disappears in the Time/Space Warp. I guess down here you call it love, but up there the Equalizer doesn't know the difference..."

I heard someone call last trip to Looneyville and the lights went out.

# 14.
# A PENTOTHAL ENEMA

I awoke hanging upside down in a harness with what looked like warm rice pudding dripping languidly through a bag into my colon. The interrogation room was white with a greasy albumin finish, and no sooner had I opened my eyes than the third degree began.

"Alright, Doolan, where did you come from and what do you want from Vice?"

The Lieutenant didn't look any smarter from this angle and my brain was unscrambled enough to know he wouldn't like my M.O. any better than before.

"I wanted some make-up tips from Sgt. Onassis here," I said, getting a swift kick in the face in exchange.

"Careful, Doolan," chimed in Saltpeter, "that's a pentothal enema. One false word and we'll know it."

"Before you went out you said something about the Equalizer. Are you some kinda amateur stereo thief, Doolan?"

"If I may Sir, the Equalizer is Death — the Great Leveller. But why dwell on that, Doolan? Shit is so much...cleaner."

This psycho babylon was starting to chafe where the bag hung and I was running low on patience. Then I heard something weird crackle out over the police band radio. Routine disturbance at a place called the Mars Bar on Avenue B. It was the name of the owner that caught my ear and spun my head, though.

Geek Pederast — a snotty delinquent I'd busted and set free for some useful information a long time ago and a whole world away. I knew if anyone down here had a lead on a twelve-year-old Martian girl or the elusive Ms. Romilar it would have to be him. If Natasha found him first, though, things wouldn't be too pleasant on the Lower East Side of his skull. Meanwhile, I had to get gone.

"The Equalizer signs my paycheck on the Red Planet."

"Then the Kremlin has its crimson tentacles in this too?"

"You got me all wrong, Comrade."

Veins started popping out on the Lieutenant's gummy forehead and rage threatened to blow a hole in the metal plate on top of his skull. He wagged a chubby finger in my face.

"You'll fry, Doolan, and that's a promise!"

I didn't hesitate. I bit two of his doughy fingers clean through and spat them like daggers right between Sgt. X's double-O's. The howls of pain from the pair of them before they lost consciousness made my blood run like molten lava.

"Get me out of this contraption or I'll wipe your ass with cold steel," I snarled at Saltpeter, and he did it. I just wish he would have washed his hands first.

Now, at least there was a glimmer of hope in this wretched panacea. When I first joined the Korps we busted a ring of small time hoods for putting acid in the water supply, then making a fortune in black-lights. I remember laughing at their greasy pompadours, but the rhythms that spilled from their transistor radio made my heart palpitate from the minute I laid ears on it.

I made sure that the kid with the crazy moniker got off with an order of experimental relocation, destination You Know Where. In return, Pederast spilled a few choice beans concerning Natashas' operation. If he was running a dive down here I figured it was high time for a nitecap, and maybe a bottom or two. To this mystery.

## 15.
## "DON'T LAUGH, YER MOTHER'S IN THE TRUNK"

Rolling through the starless night, tape deck pumping brutal noise, the Martians mused on the strange hand fate had dealt them. That is, if 'muse' is the proper term for shooting up cocaine, hanging moons out the window and screaming at the top of your lungs.

All-American phrases like 'bitchin' and 'damn the torpedoes' were tossed around as often as 'where the fukk are we?' and 'Suzy isn't breathing anymore.' It didn't hurt that by now they'd had time to sample the creature comforts of their dead hosts' mobile playpen. The black velvet bar and billiard nook served as a makeshift conference room for the band, their manager, and the girls as Gizmo rolled the semi down a lonely stretch of what used to be Route 66. For once the conversation turned to music, sort of, when Atom said —

"Did you see these guys' itinerary yet? They've got a show in New York the day after tomorrow."

"We don't know any songs yet, how we gonna play a show?"

Off in the corner, Trash watched Eddie penetrate Angel with a pool cue and waited for an answer. The life of a drummer is a sick and sordid affair. Constant pounding of the skins sets the tempo for nightly dominance rituals that all too often end in a puddle of Black Label beer and the squeals of some dim oinkette ringing through the tissue paper walls of a local squathouse. And that was just how Trash liked it.

Now that the initial euphoria of the Time/Space Warp had worn off, he tried wrapping his pea-sized cranium around the sticky whys and wherefores of space travel, car-jacking and manslaughter. That took all of 45 seconds. In the background, Angel more bellowed than moaned as Eddie opened a beer through the miracle of **vagina dentata**.

"We can always have those two do their thing while I read poetry. We'll call it Erotic Performance Art," said Buckley.

Never one to doubt he and his buddies non-existent talents, Atom had another idea.

"Fukk the dumb shit, I'll write us a song. This van is fully wired for sound and we can rehearse it on the way to New York. We're gonna do that fukkin' show on Saturday!"

Suzy had been passed out for most of the ride, but she woke up and raised her eyelids with effort. Downers and wine were a bad combination for day dreaming.

"You guys can't play anything, you can barely play with yourselves."

Atom went to slap her, but she'd passed out again.

"We can do it, it'll be easy. Look at Jesus, he couldn't carry a tune."

"How about this," broke in Buckley, always the clueless optimist, "you guys get out on stage... the houselights go up, the crowd screams, anticipation thick in the air...then BAM! A half hour of total silence. It's stark, simple, effective...and it's Art!"

A shower of beer, a kick to the groin and the matter was settled. Angel and Eddie slumped to the floor in a bovine heap.

Atom and Trash were still dreaming of naked women, day-glo body paint and a bigger piece of tomorrow.

# 16.
# BLOOD AND SODA POP

"I'm famished, darling. Let's stop for a bite."

Natasha steered her faithful pet into a dirty corner grocery. Entranced by the rows of unhealthy food, she sauntered transfixed up one aisle and down the next. Faust spied a group of Hispanic teenagers staring and pointing at them, but Natasha was oblivious.

"Oh, look, an old-fashioned whipped cream dispenser, can you imagine?"

She took a drag off the can and her knees buckled, eyes rolling back in her head. The floor and ceiling spun like a roulette wheel, offering the only escape her rancid psyche would ever know. But it was brief, always too brief. When she came to, a Puerto Rican youth was brandishing a handful of fruit at her and smiling broadly as she lay on the floor.

"You want some nice mangoes, huh, lady?"

Natasha viewed the young man with interest. He was olive skinned and the scent of salsa turned bad wafted off of him as he limped toward her, khaki pants covering his legs like vines. Miss Thing just licked her lips absently —

"And your testicles look absolutely gargantuan in those tight ethnic trousers."

Natasha was pulled hard to her feet, but she never went limp. Faust didn't miss a beat either.

"Insolent whelp," he said, zapping the challenger with ten thousand volts from his fake arm.

The boy turned to mush and death was instant. When it's my turn to go I want it just as quick. I also want plastic flowers and front row center at Gilligan's Wake.

Meanwhile, the gang exchanged guttural Spanish and quizzical looks. As a rule their females took abuse much better than they dished it out, Venus as Mars.

"Oh darling, you mustn't," Natasha said to Faust with a gleam in her eye. "They're so... swarthy."

Slowly, deliberately, one of the gang pulled out a large stiletto. He eyed the pair, a jones for vengeance etched on his baby face.

"Fukk this pincé midget and this fukking puta beech!"

Faust aimed a can of refried beans at the boy's temple and he too lay dead, decapitated on the floor.

Natasha let out a roar of throaty good cheer and put her spiked heel in a wanting jugular vein. Blood spurted like soda pop from a shaken can. Faust used his head and his height to good advantage, skull-butting gonads with obvious relish. When the skirmish was over, bodies and broken glass lay scattered everywhere.

Two frightened old men emerged from behind the counter. One held a sawed-off shotgun, his knuckles trembling white.

But, a group of urban bikers had been watching the scene unfold from outside. They disarmed the shopkeeper, grabbing his gun and filling their pockets with junk food and beer. A hulking bear of a man approached Natasha and Faust, surveyed the thrashed and wounded bodies struggling to their feet, and laughed out loud.

"These bean-eaters bugging you, precious?"

"Heavens, no. They're charming."

Her carnal interest in the Hispanics had been quickly replaced by this new group of greasy misfits, especially one limbless stump in battle fatigues who rode on a wooden plank with wheels.

"And who is this deviated specimen?" she asked, stroking the long, viscous hair that snaked down his shoulders.

"That's Bobo the Vet, sweetheart, the terror of Pan Moon Jong. I'm Elmo, Grand Dragon of the Hells Harlots Motorcycle Club."

At that moment, a blue light went on behind Natasha's black eyes and a plan began to take root in her twisted mind.

# 17.
## VAUDEVILLE ONLY HINTED

The Mars Bar was a seedy two story brownstone affair with a red neon sign on the outside. I'm not the most sociable guy in the galaxy, and to tell the truth, these kinds of places always make me want to change species. There's nothing like a couple of million miles and a mission to put you in the mood, though. Without a warning, a spikey head in a leather jacket bum rushed through the swinging doors and square into yours truly.

"Say cat, is this the Mars Bar?"

"Oh fukk, I feel like shit, I think I'm gonna puke."

"Well, make up your mind kid, you're confusing me."

The kid looked up, bewildered, his big mouth hanging open like an Egyptian tomb. By the looks of him he'd barely escaped puberty, but already a history of mankinds' dullness had carved its way onto his cold pizza face.

"I don't fukkin' know... I feel real shitty..." his head lolled from side to side, "and if I don't puke soon, I think I'm gonna die."

"Say, you're a real renaissance pig, ain'tcha?"

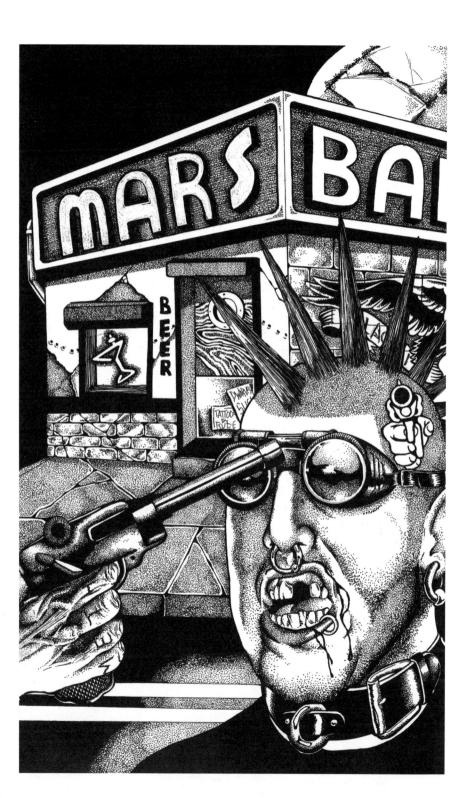

At that the punk seemed to take notice of me for the first time. Reeling on spindly legs he looked me up and down with a sneer. Putrid as his personality seemed, I had the universal alien jones to talk too much, to whoever. He also looked like he might be able to score for some crank.

"Fukk off, ya rancid slice of headcheese. I'm here to get some skank."

He tried to push by me, but I was running low on good sportsmanship. I grabbed him by the neck of his strategically ripped t-shirt and popped the question —

"The owner of this dump, he wouldn't happen to be a mug with a chest like a deflated water balloon and a tattoo of $E=mc^2$ on it, would he?"

The silence was deafening, but the quiver on the punk's downy lip told the whole sad story.

"You may be in over your circumspective head junior, 'cause that's Geek Pederast. He claims that his peter's a holy flesh crucible, known to lure stupid kids, hairdressers and other New York artists to sleazy holes like this one. Only one false move and they go from Times Square to where time and space are squared and vaudeville only hinted at."

I guess I lost my mind in the verbiage, but I wanted this stringbean to savvy before it was too goddamn late for him. He just looked at me slightly psycho and said —

"You're a fascist...you're a creep...you're an asshole."

"Simmer down you little weasel, you'll muss your D.A."

"D.A.? Motherfukker's got nothing on me."

"I mean your hairdo, daddio. It's really bitchin'."

The punk got a weird glint in his eye like an amphetamine blowfish in a shooting gallery. He started to ease away from me, disgust clouding his acneed mug.

"Holy shit! You're a queer, I'm calling a cop."

"I am a cop."

"I'm calling a straight one then."

That one snapped me back to the here and now. I'd had enough of the New York heat to last me a lifetime, and I didn't want this little miscreant to think I was some kind of nervous nellie. I figured on smoothing things over with him.

"Look kid, be a sport. I'll buy you a root beer and we'll throw some Elvis on the nickelodeon."

"Elvis? That bloated capitalist shitheel? Guys like him ruin rock 'n' roll."

That tore it. Like a lesbian track star's hamstrings, that tore it. I saw red, white and purple and I punched the little fukker hard in the throat. We traded knuckles for awhile, me getting in five or six for every lame attempt from his corner.

I thought about Elvis, the once and future Thing, eating bacon with peanut butter and worshipping his mommy. Now that's rock 'n' roll. I was holding the kid up with the force of my blows and I knew I should quit before he woke up dead. Instead, I took out the old Fly-Rite and started to strangle him with it.

Warm ooze trickled down my fingers and I saw a knifeblade glinting in the grimey sun. Whether he was slicing for the yo-yo or my ding-a-ling, we'll never know. The bang from my Luger was deafening.

## 18.
## BOLOGNA SANDWICHES AND AN ENEMA BAG

"You shot him," she said, and I had to admit she was right. Nothing gets past these Earth women.

"I don't think I hurt him too bad, his pants are still dry."

Whatever passed for normal conversation in this joint resumed as two throwback doormen bounced the stiff out of the doorway and onto the sidewalk. I guess you see that sort of thing all the time in this town. At least I had some young nubile's attention. She looked good, but not too good. Sort of a cross between Annette Funicello and Vampira.

"Care to dance, dollface?"

"I can't. Dancing brings too much oxygen to my brain."

Goddamn, shut down again. Seems like every move you make around here lands you in the deep freeze. Still, she wasn't leaving and that's always part one. Part two came when she said —

"Wanna line?"

Caramba! This little floozy was talking my language now. She spread two thick rails on the sloppy bar top and it was more than I could do to keep from

snorting both of them and downing her margarita, little pink umbrella and all. The meth dripped down my throat and into my bloodstream sending rhythmic arcs of light and shadow pulsing through my brain.

As I stared at the cracks in the ceiling I realized I was flat on my back again. Revived by a bucket of suds, I felt just a twinge of remorse for my habits. At the end of the day though, they were the only things I could count on.

This planet was something else again. A harlot on every corner and nothing on the jukebox. But, somewhere down here there was a Martian girl with my name on her lips and nowhere to go but straight downward.

The skirt was on fire as she helped me to my feet and dusted me off. Fluorescent light played with the beginnings of crows feet and disillusion tugged at the corners of her face.

"Listen, do you think you could do me a favor?"

I could think of about a dozen, only a few of which included farm implements and Krisco, but she had other ideas.

"Could you kill me too? I tried it once, and I'm not sure if it worked or not, but it really turned me on."

Well didn't that beat all? Here she was, hot and cool and anything in between, with everything to live for. Everything but the will. I could still see a brighter tomorrow for us, starlight streaming through crushed velour curtains as we bred the beast with two backs and a gizzard.

"Couldn't we pack a few bologna sandwiches and an enema bag and get back to nature instead?"

"I'd rather die."

She came over all peaceful like a hooker at a funeral and I pumped three in her gut. What the hell, I hate hip girls anyway.

# 19.
# THE LONG HELLO

"Who the fukk is blowing away my hyper-chic clientele...Doolan!"

"Been a long time, Pederast."

"Longer than it was hard, Doolan, ya flimsy meteor maid."

Jesus, did we sound that goofy in real life? Conversing with the Gotham City disco crowd had me nervous about my colorful phrasemaking, but hearing it from the Geek almost got me homesick, and that too was trouble. For the both of us.

"Save the long hellos, Balzac. Natasha and that righteous runt Faust are here in your oily little backyard. You can help me find them or die trying."

All the piss and vinegar drained from his milky white face. He'd dropped a dime on Mars' Pubic Enemy #1 once and only fate's fickle digits had left him respiratory this long. I knew he'd crumble like week-old coffee cake.

"She'll have my hide if she finds me," he said, lips quivering like Pavarotti's sternum.

"You'll be lucky if she lets it go at that, Pederast. Remember the Dion quintuplets? There used to be two of them."

I didn't know what that meant exactly, but I kind of liked watching his shorts spring a leak. The fear of God always takes a back seat to the menace of womanhood.

"You gotta save me, Doolan. You... you got me into this."

"I don't have to do a damn thing but eat, sleep and reproduce in that order. Natasha doesn't know you're down here yet, and as long as you cooperate, it'll stay that way. Meanwhile, you're sporting a liquor license, which means you're paying off somebody. If the heat comes around asking questions about me, you're deaf, dumb and ugly. And if your morbid clientele starts tripping on any new designer substances, find me some names and locales. Just don't forget the free samples."

I left through the door, but I'd found the proverbial gutter. Here, where the cruel stench of terror and three-day-old beer lingered, that was where I'd find Suzy, and we'd finish this snake dance for good.

## 20.
# INTRAVENOUS VERITAS

Natasha was breaking immutable laws of physics right and left as she contorted, gratifying a horde of hopped-up bikers on the floor of their drug-lab/clubhouse/crime scene. Except for the absence of blood and severed limbs it looked a lot like the aftermath of the 'Grocery Store Massacre', as the local tabloids had dubbed it. Faust made finger sandwiches while getting a rim-job from a hag they called Mama Beloo.

As bikers staggered bleary from the fray, their fearless leader Elmo stood tongue-tied, not sure if he and the Harlots were caught in a dream or trapped in a nightmare.

"Natasha, you are one hot bitch."

"Thank you, Elmo. Are your men having any luck peddling that morphine and helium derivative I've synthesized?"

She cooked up a generous helping and jammed the hypodermic, point first into her left eye.

"The neighborhood brats like it so much we're already swimming in milk money. And if they try and get cute, we pawn their vintage lunchboxes."

Natasha paused to ruminate on a world gone bad. She'd always heard that Earth might be the last out-

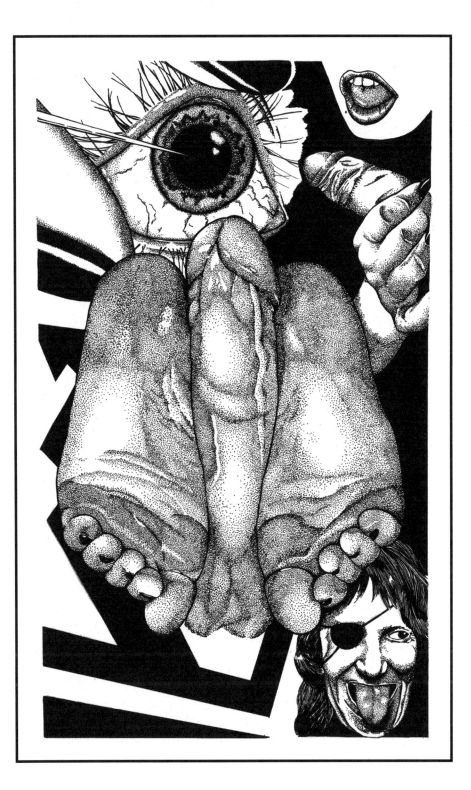

post of arcane morality in the cosmos, but she knew now that was just a veneer, a wistful dream from days gone by. In fact, the degradation of this little world was maybe that much more sublime for the illusions that its people clung to like a worn-out teet.

"Are there really millions of sociopaths like you on this planet, Elmo?" she asked.

But, he was on the phone screaming at someone over a deal gone bad. Natasha turned the radio up, her long white fingers drawn to her lap like gypsy moths to a flame.

"Our time will come," she thought.

## 21.
# BEEF JERKY AND CHICLETS

The band pulled off of the turnpike and onto a gravel parking lot in front of two signs, one of which said 'GAS,' the other 'EAT.' The irony was lost on them. Spilling out of the semi they stretched their legs and took in their surroundings. Flat, treeless prairie as far as the Martian eye could see.

A bunch of truckers in matching baseball caps emerged from the restaurant. They spotted the group standing by the semi and ambled over, spitting tobacco. One dull-eyed, bad old boy looked the band up and down and smiled, his vacant glare coming to rest on Suzy's microscopic halter top.

"You're gonna catch your death o' cold, little lady."

The other truckers snickered, kicking clods of dirt with their workboots. Menace hung like beef from a hook.

"And you fellas look like you could use a haircut."

The next to speak was a visibly nervous Buckley. He didn't like violence if there was any way to avoid it, and now that the band had tasted blood he wanted to keep the body count to a minimum.

"You know, you're right. We had much better hair last tour."

With hatred thick in the mid-western air the truckers came towards them. Gizmo let out an interplanetary war-whoop. Aside from killing that metal band, this was gonna be the only fun he'd had down here yet.

Unfortunately, for the Okies, they didn't know what 'red-neck' meant until they'd fukked with a bunch of Martians.

The asphalt cowboys lost limbs, eyes, testicles and everything else in the brawl that ensued. Flannel arms ripped from sockets as though they belonged to mannequins, blood flowed and hideous shrieks filled the nighttime sky.

For the truckers death came swiftly, like everyone should come. The ringleader lay motionless on the ground, his blackened heart ripped out and a plug of tobacco turned deep crimson in the corner of his mouth. Trash toyed with the notion of eating him, but settled instead on a breakfast of beef jerky and Chiclets.

The gravitational pull of Earth being what it is, the strength and agility of Lucifers Crank were superhuman. How they managed to breathe in an oxygen based atmosphere had something to do with the adaptability of people in their profession, and the fact that they never stopped drinking long enough to give it much thought.

## 22.
# EROTIC TINCTURE ENGINEERS

Twelve hours later, Lucifers Crank pulled up to the Mars Bar, adrenaline running high. Between bitter feuding and reckless drug consumption they'd written a song and almost had it down. As long as their performance incited an immediate riot they wouldn't even need any more material. The semi ground to halt and a gnomelike, ageless man in a satin tour jacket was upon them.

"Like, why the delay, hombrés? We were starting to bug."

"Just a little trouble in the desert," said Buckley, terrified that the afternoon papers would be full of mug shots of the aliens who had killed a heavy metal band and hijacked their career.

"That's some heavy shit. You guys don't look so good."

"We're changing images," said Eddie, to end the conversation. It wasn't over.

"The naked bitches and day-glo paint are in your dressing room."

"Naked what?" asked Suzy.

The entire band had now entered the auditorium. Before the girls knew what was happening, the stage

manager had closed and bolted the door in front of them. The girls were locked out. Suzy looked at Angel — the older, harder, dumber version of herself. Although they had bosoms, they were far from buddies as they made eye contact for the first time since they had met. Angel let out a noncommittal —

"Fukk."

Was that a threat or an invitation? Suzy-Q's short life passed before her open eyes. The dark shadows of school and church, the briney tentacles of her nuclear family; she saw the whole planet hurtling fast toward a brick, earthen wall.

"Cool," she said.

A battered Impala pulled up with a pimply driver at the wheel. On its ermine mudflaps the letters "IB" were stencilled. It took 'Hungry' Jack McKay all of three seconds to size up the situation and make his move.

"Ladies, I represent a local eatery and escort service. May I take you for a ride?"

## 23.
# ROSE AND THE RED PLANET

I took my leave of the Mars Bar and hit the street. Little red fireworks went off behind my eyelids as I stopped and waited for my brain to catch up to the inside of my skull. A girl was standing in an alleyway a few doors down from the bar, thirteen if she was a day, sporting two blond pig-tails and a bright red ribbon around her corsetted waist.

"Wanna date?"

"I don't care much for health food."

Night after night I walked the gamey boulevard alone in the rain. Sometimes it seemed like the whores owned Metropolis, with those god awful pockmarks gouged on their faces. There were red ones, white ones, blue or turning blue.

And then I saw what looked like an apparition in vinyl and lipgloss. I didn't doubt she was bad news, but one quick look put a handful of ripe plantains in my hip pocket. She was an Amazon woman alright, the kind that can pump you to a glandular frenzy while she fixes a cold roast beef and slits your jugular vein. Under that phosphorescent streetlight she gave a déja view of Natasha and me in happier times and...well, you get the bullet, point first. She clinched it when she asked me —

"Are you lonesome tonight?"

The first thing I noticed in the flea-bag hotel room was magic fingers on the bed, so while she douched over the ice bucket I tried them on for size. They threw me clear across the room, and as I sat picking shards of broken mirror from my scalp she emerged wearing a see-through teddy with lace garters and enough lipstick to mark the Vienna Boys Choir for life. She also had a tattoo of a rose and the Red Planet.

"You've been a very bad boy," she said, pointing to the jagged scars that criss-crossed a painfully white body.

My fly unzipped itself and I felt the ointment rising in my loins. Her eyes got wide and she made as if to faint, but instead she let out a sap curdling shriek and bolted for the window, crashing through the glass and into the street. I looked down at Doolan Junior. I guess everything is a little bigger· on Mars.

"There's always gland to hand combat," I thought, thumbing through a Gideon Bible for inspiration.

"It is better to spill thine seed on the belly of a whore..."

No doubt about that one. I flipped on the TV.

It was through the miracle of the soft-core nudie channel that I found my next clue. An advertisement in the classic smiling moron vein, but with a twist that told you that the future was now and tomorrow was gonna be a king-sized drag.

It seemed that some wily entrepreneur had found a way to make the world's oldest profession accessible to the working class drone. It was called the Intercourse Barn, a fastmeat brothel. I guess nothing is sacred when you're naked, but the addition of special sauce to the sex act was one that I knew planet Earth could do without.

One of the young lovelies on the screen was what caught my attrition, though. I couldn't be sure, but even with ten pounds of makeup and hosiery on, she still looked like the EQ's one and only daughter. I got dressed in a hurry and left the room through the window, licking my wounds. Like a queen in a henhouse, I had to get straight.

## 24.
# ELEVEN YEARS DEAD

Ten jags of powdered coffee later, I'm back on my flophouse bed with a mad dagger in my soul. Perusal of the radio yielded nothing with a backbeat. The room smelled of spilled rum and synthetic coke, mildew and bats' piss. I'd paced the carpet until I'd left footprints.

Why had Suzy-Q and those two-bit punks vanished like dinosaurs in a tar-pit, and how could she have gone so wrong, so fast? And where did Natasha fit into the equation? I was sure she was dead. As dead as this planet I'd thought I could trip on, this extra-terrestrial void with a bad case of chicken malaise.

Polluted as Earth was though, my head was that much dirtier. I heard a sound like an Edsel hovercraft and a crash through the window brought my drunken reverie to a screeching halt.

A kid about eleven years dead was lying on my floor in a pool of blood and broken glass. He said from the speckled linoleum —

"Don't move or I'll blow your fukking gourd off! Gimme all your money."

"Money? I'm a cop."

"Then give me two tickets to the Policeman's Ball."

Every slacker's a comic on this godforsaken orb. I checked out his arms. He had track marks the size of golf tees and a homemade tattoo of $E=mc^2$. The plot got so thick I could eat it on crackers.

"We're on the 99th floor, Pee-Wee. How come you're crashing my window party?"

"The Space-Lady gave me a shot."

"Space-Lady?"

"Yeah, she's really neat. She's got a pet midget and he made the whole Sunday School disappear!"

Faust, that little he-goat. I'd noticed when the kid had smashed through the window that something had fallen out of his pocket. I picked it up and peeped an ad for a show going on that night at Pederast's place, the Mars Bar. The poster showed a bunch of guys with pancake make-up and high heeled shoes on. I gathered that this was what they called rock 'n' roll now and it turned my stomach.

"You gonna make this freak scene, squirt?"

"Yeah, everybody's going. Everybody who's antibody."

"Alright Tarzan, the stairs are out the door and to your left. Now scram."

"I'll take the elevator copper," he said dramatically, and dropped like a nickel balloon.

In space no one hears you scream. Of course, on Earth it's a little bit different. My mind drifted back to the end of the last chapter.

The Intercourse Barn? Be still my snaking hard.

# 25.
# THE INTERCOURSE BARN

"Good evening and welcome to the Intercourse Barn. I'm Hungry Jack, your mack dad in training."

"I'm not hankering for pink Zorro, just looking for that certain someone."

"No need to be bashful here, sir, a little anonymous companionship never hurt anyone. And if it did, well that's five bucks extra."

The Intercourse Barn. The world's first house of ill repute based on fast food marketing principles and a never-ending supply of comely tarts in the labor pool. Talk about your entry-level debauchery though, a hard-on seemed as unlikely here as the life sized portrait of Iceberg Slim with his nads in the deep fryer that hung on the faux velvet wallpaper.

"Look pal, I didn't come here for S&M Green Stamps..."

The fancy patter was starting to wear on my nerves, so I grabbed a hold of the oversize collar of his polyester pimp coat and gave a healthy yank. The scent of Aqua Velva played off chartreuse fringe and a personalized nameplate.

"I'm looking for a girl about twelve years old with peachy freckles and a size 00 brassiere."

"She's tied up at the moment, how about Li'l Anna Rexie, the best in petite passions? No teeth left, but a great personality. Or, if pain is your pleasure, why not take a stab at Pinky Slim? She's got Lou Gherig's Disease and she's willing to share."

Oh, Lordy; what kind of a greasy womb had I slid into this time? Was this guy pulling my leg or yanking my chain? And why had I once again tempted the e-coli call of carnality?

I guess because the business of pleasure's a rough one, no quarter asked without two dimes and a nickel in return. And it wasn't over yet, not by a long shot.

"If you can't decide on a whole one, why not sample our 'A La Parte' menu, sir?"

"A La Parte?"

"Mix and match exotic genitalia at our Pornocopia Buffet. It's a real mess o' satisfying passions for the man on the go. After all, you deserve a break — from the rest of her."

Now, I wasn't always known as Mr. Sensitive back in the trenches, but I'd come to understand the value of estrogen, sometimes even the price of it. I conjured the spirit of Amelia Dairy Airheart, stuck my Luger in the little ferret's mouth and cocked it.

"For a nickel, I'd blow your swollen head off."

"For a dime, I'm authorized to swallow the bullet."

I pulled the trigger to thunderous internal applause. An avalanche of horse-faced glamorettes exited screaming from the back room, followed in short order by an army of lunch-hour Romeos shielding their faces and pulling their drawers up.

Then, razed and confused, looking like a rag-trade cover girl came Suzy-Q. Her lips were black and crimson, her hair teased up in a ratty B-five-2, but the final effect left no doubt she was cradlebait. If I'd ever wondered what kind of a twisted wreck could lust after one so young and obliging I suddenly saw the rearview mirror turned directly on yours truly, and I felt the kind of lurid desire that no one but that certain fatal femme had ever aroused before.

"You bastard! Jack was my inside guy. He was gonna get me a job on the line."

"With friends like that, doll, who needs enemas?"

She teetered on razor-sharp heels for a second, peeped through my looking-glass hormones. You could fill a burning chasm with what she knew, and I knew she knew. She was older than springtime and too high to care.

As she merged with the lipstick stampede I had the urge to tell her my feelings for her were far from paternal, but strategy dictated otherwise. If she'd wound up at this juke joint, she must have been heaved from that retard glee-club's passion posse.

A sweet young thing alone and headless on a strange and diabolical planet, nothing but cannon fodder — goodbye cruel world. I thought about chasing her down, but I figured she'd wind up at the Mars Bar tonight looking for romantic retribution. And she wouldn't be alone.

## 26.
# STRAFED BY AN UGLY STICK

New York in the evening is a whore with wings, all lit up like a debutante's mom — ripe, rotten for the picking. There were no more clues to confuse me, just the night and the stars you couldn't see, but you knew they were there.

At this stage of the game there are three things I can't abide: men, women and children. Drugs on Earth weren't better, there were just more of them and everywhere you looked people threw their insides out at you. The lights went off behind my eyeballs and I came over all rancho-cathartic, Seig Heil for the call of the wild.

It was time to get back to my mission position. Find Suzy or die trying, both would be too much to hope for. I had the time and space, what I needed now was the ammunition, bystanders be damned. No one is innocent.

The Mars Bar perched on the grey Manhattan skyline, daring pigeons to do their damndest. Teenage hipsters — pierced, scarred and strafed by an ugly stick, pushed through the big iron doors past bouncers so dumb they just had to be real. The women looked good, they always do. In fact, the closer I got the more I detected generous helpings of summertime flesh and a hot flash like menopause overtook me.

"Face it, Doolan. You don't have the duds, you

can't speak the lingo, and goddamnit, you're all out of crank. You couldn't score in this freak scene without professional help."

My self-inflicted stalemate was broken by Pederast, who came running out the door at warp speed.

"Doolan, you son of a bitch," he said, without a hint of nostalgia, "Natasha just ordered a Cuervo and antifreeze. She'll have my balls if she makes me!"

"Since when are your orbitals different than everybody else's?" I thought, as wistfully as you can think about a woman who eats glass for breakfast and prune juice at lunch.

"For Christ's sake, she's selling dope to the skater rats."

"I never knew her to give it away free, Einstein."

My eyes were two UFOs in a sea of red licorice, the back of my throat like a methadone tar-pit. And Pederast was just a sick puppy with mange of the cranium.

"What kind of a pig are you now, Doolan?"

"The kind without a city, without a country, without a planet. The kind without a badge, without a stick, without a dog, without a prayer... and here's a little something I've been saving up for you."

I gave him three slugs from the Luger. The crowd

broke and ran, but I knew Pederast would pull through alright. He was yellow, but his blood ran Martian green. The doormen parted like Moses at Alfalfa's pompadour.

## 27.
# A FIFTH OF OBLIVION

"What delightful sport, Faust. These painted ladies are stunning."

"Indeed..." he said, slathering finger paint on a firm ass cheek and slapping it smartly.

The members of Lucifers Crank hadn't quite had their fill of watching naked women covered in paint cavort around their dressing room, but the fifth of oblivion the Mars Bar had provided looked pale compared to the helium fortified bug-juice 'Big Mama' Romilar and the Hells Harlots were dishing out. Of course, once the dope took hold the bikers had their own, not so abstract plans for the objects d'art.

A bottle blond, her mouth filled to overflowing by a zircon retainer, pawed at her haunches in a heap of mink and pigment. Somebody's kid sister was tying her arm off as Natasha eyed bulging veins like a lynx in heat.

"You like this, it excites you?"

"It helps me express myself," she said, staring at her life's blood as it clogged up the tube below the rubber stopper.

Meanwhile, a crowd had gathered outside of the Mars Bar, and as Geek Pederast miraculously got to his feet, the men of Precinct 5-0 came on the scene in a

puff of Brylcream and ignorance. Lt. Grizzle spoke for a generation of swine.

"Holy shit!"

"No word yet on the papal potty visit, but new evidence suggests fecal worship as early as Thomas Aquinas."

It was Sgt. Saltpeter, always quick with his two shits, and bringing up the rear was Sgt. X, looking stunned in a sheer negligée over shapeless corduroy culottes. He'd come in such a blinding flash of speed that he'd barely had time to accessorize.

"Tell us who done this to you! Who shot you down dead like a dog in the street?"

Pederast was shaken, not stirred, all Bozo and George Raft as he spat —

"His name's Doolan, but he won't fry, he's the heat."

"Oh, he's something hot alright. And it just hit the fan!"

# 28.
# MAYHEM & THE BEAT

I drew my gun, and more for the fukk of it than anything else started popping caps at random. The anticipated jerk-off stampede never materialized, though. Maybe they thought it was an art piece I was firing.

Lucifers Crank took the stage in a hail of beer cans and bad vibrations. The whole crowd seemed amped for a Texas brawl, bodies flying through the air even before a note was sounded. The smell of hairspray and homicide hung thick in the night and something told me shoot first, ask questions never. I thought I saw Suzy disappearing backstage, but I couldn't be sure with the lights and the smoke from my gun. Big chords beat at my chest like the surf at a blood bank.

The song was called "Teenagers From Mars" and at least you knew that they meant it. The crowd became a mob with ticket stubs, having their way with the hall. No rules, no order, just mayhem and the beat as the living corpses swelled against the stage in a frenzy as dark as the lid of a country coffin.

Then the speed overtook me again. I saw myself — a spirit of flesh, hot as an oven, burning away. The music turned light and transparent, the crowd a field of dandelions, each soul a head to be popped. I fired blindly; bodies fell, meaningful glances instantly death throes. The front of the stage and my Luger loomed large. I felt my mind snap, but my body forged

on toward naked daylight and the land of free cocktails.

The wall of humanity was so thick I could barely move, but I was close enough to see Suzy-Q enter through the Members Only doorway with matrimonial warfare etched on her face. I gave a mighty heave forward and fell in not three feet from the action, just in time to see her double-take as she spotted Natasha and Faust at the center of their grimey tableau. She tried to escape, but her way was blocked by two writhing bodies, long enough for Faust to ask —

"Equalizer's daughter...artistic discipline...delicious...seize her..."

In a heartbeat Suzy was naked and covered in paint. I sprang to attention, so hard I almost split a seam. Her tiny frame called to mind afternoons spent in my sweltering adolescent crawlspace drooling over a dog-eared copy of *The Diary of Anne Frank*.

Natasha appraised her victim coldly, but not without hatred.

"Your father is a man whom I loathe beyond measure, whom I've sworn to destroy by any means necessary."

If this was meant to alarm Suzy, she didn't show it. On the contrary, she seemed glad that someone else shared her fatal vision of the old man.

"That was the last thing my mother said, before she joined the flea circus."

Natasha couldn't speak for one long moment; recognition, then confusion crossed her face, but didn't know where to land. Finally, she struck a harsh blow to Suzy's sternum, knocking her windless.

"Save your breath, darling. Elmo, you and the others tie her to the ceiling."

## 29.
# EVERYTHING HAPPENS AT ONCE

When everything happens at once there's no one to blame but the weather. You couldn't argue with my entrance though, guns blazing a South Side lullaby, the soft shoe a Florsheim to the gullet. There was no taming the blood jones I'd been keeping in check.

I heard gun fire to my right and saw New York's Swinest closing flanks and capping innocent bystanders like a mad case of civil unrest. As usual, The People couldn't help but be anywhere that wasn't in the line of fire.

The Hells Harlots heaved the better part of a toolchest at me piece by agonizing piece, still I couldn't keep my eyes off the tender morsels dressed in paint and nothing but. Slugs sang make hay while the sun shines and bad moons rose.

In a makeshift harness Suzy-Q was lifted toward the ceiling, young legs spread wide for the first assault. I saw bikers filling huge burlesque-sized syringes, banging up and slowly rising off the floor toward the prepubescent promised land.

If you've never been hit on the head with a lead pipe it's a sensation I'd have to recommend. You're never so much one with the Earth as when the floor rushes up to meet your face like an old friend. I guess seeing Natasha up close and personal in glorious black and white was about the only thing that could still make me concussion nostalgic. That was how we'd said goodbye the last time.

This time around it was all business, Martian style, straight from the old Korps manual —

"Natasha Romilar, you have the right to remain violent. Everything you do can, and will be imitated five years later on television. If you want an attorney you're out of your mind, but I can get you carpeting wholesale. Any questions?"

"Darling, how can anyone take you seriously with that loathsome fedora on?"

My first instinct was the cold-blooded murder of Natasha, Faust, the Cro-Mag bikers and everything else that wasn't nailed down. It just had to be done with style. I pulled out the Fly-Rite and walked the dog across two dimpled foreheads. They dropped.

I lassoed Faust's wrist with the razor wire, his screams a symphony, then shot two gravity defying dirtbags who popped intestines and fell to the floor like lead balloons. Suzy's precarious cherry would be safe for the moment. My Luger spat brimstone.

The men of Precinct 5-0 made it backstage finally, only to get caught in the crossfire of the bikers' AK-47s. Sgt. X was the first to fall, his frilly lingerie a dark red tangle beneath the lonesome corduroy. Lt. Grizzle took a slug to the belly, adding second-hand donuts and bile to the remains of the bands' obligatory deli tray.

Sgt. Saltpeter's only attempt at self-defense was his patented two-ply Kleenex bulletproof vest. Like his whole career in law enforcement it was a rousing failure, a waste of blood and tissue.

For me, hot pursuit was an understatement, what with Natasha, backfield in motion, so close you could taste her with your stomach. We careened through a maze of dark hallways, the intestines of the joint, and I felt the familiar throb of my johnson chafing the rough of my pants. Girls like this you don't get, though. The best you can hope for is a stand-off and maybe carfare.

Jesus leapt.

What followed was a catfight with me as the unfortunate rodent. Quick as I could, I sized up the situation. I was weak and looped on goofers. She was a glandular Jackson, the tourniquet round my wanting neck. Give me the big one, the Last Hurrah, with tears streaming and Satan hovering in the foreground.

But, the Good Lord hates a mercy killing, and sometimes the Fat Lady gets ham in her windpipe. Natasha got very quiet all of a sudden, but her body was taut like a highwire.

## 30.
## GRATUITOUS VIVA L'AMOURE IN MONOXIDE BLACK

Natasha took my all-too-human fly down and gripped me firmly, the dry pulse of her hand exquisitely painful. The tip of her tongue played around the edge of my root, here lightly like the silkworm, there molten like a pail of warm glue.

With much wailing and gnashing of hair what followed was one for the vaults, an exercise in gratuitous viva l'amoure that would bury any ten on your planet no matter what they might yap by the henhouse door.

These are dark days for cocksparring women and nobody fought the good fight like the raging Ms. Romilar. They say it's always better to regret something you have done than to regret something you haven't. As I fell away unconscious I could feel the venom trickle out of her.

Was I gone for an instant, an hour, an eon? The next time I opened my eyes it was carnage American style. Natasha had flipped her libidinous wig, and clothed in nothing but monoxide black hair and a nonexistent bikini line she was vaporizing the entire crowd with that monstrous Martian death warp. A mad look like a dog with green saliva engorged her eyes, and no mere mortal could have hoped to put a dent in that plan of pure evil.

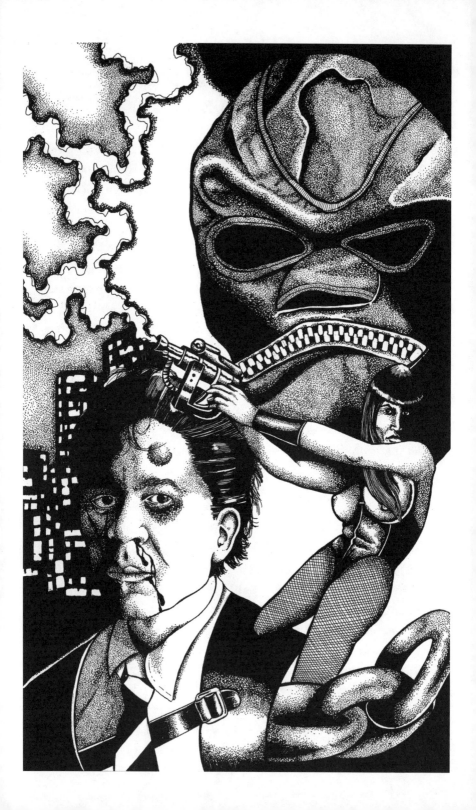

Locals, yokels and wild ones alike felt the antiseptic sting of the Time/Space Warp, and if they thought they were alienated already, they didn't know the half of it. Lucifers Crank kept rocking the two chords that defined an evening of chaos and perversion, but as pockets of screaming teens ascended toward the astral homeland, even the bands' dope-addled minds started to click.

Riding on a roar of destructive applause, Eddie unslung his bass and heaved it at Natasha. As quickly as the guitar was thrown, though, Faust had hurled himself into its path. The angle was such that he couldn't see Natasha blasting back at the stage with the warp ray and, in a sickening instant, the dwarf was history.

If the last half-hour had been Purgatory, this development screamed welcome to Hell. Natasha instantly became a naked dervish spitting vile invective at a who-cares moon. Faust was her lover, her dog, her reason for being, and now he was gone.

If I were religious I might have said a rosary, but as it was I made it an open letter to the Patron Saint of Hiroshima. Nothing would stop Natasha from having revenge on The Crank, on your humble narrator, and on the very orb you call home.

As I braced for the worst, visions of Suzy's plumb danced in my head. I guess I realized then what my Holy Grail was and for once, instead of cursing fate, I counted blessings. The right side was up, the up side was down, and if it ended here, well then so be it.

I'd never seen the Reaper effect a specimen like Natasha before, her pathology so round, so firm, so fully packed; but I don't know what else it could have been that rang down the curtain on our last installment. She glared at me, the familiar malice in her eyes, and though she had me like a deer in her headlights she didn't aim the highbeams at me or even at the Great Unwashed.

Slowly, determined to enjoy every spine tapping second, she undulated like a world weary reptile to a tune that no one could hear. Then, she turned the Time/Space Warp on herself and made the big leap to another, hotter Eden.

# 31.
## WE ROASTED WEENIES ON
## THE FUNERAL PYRE

Saturday morning.

The New York sky looks a little greener, the sidewalk's hot with crunchy locusts and God is dead in his heaven. Suzy hasn't been home for a week and a half. I didn't notice until this morning, so I guess it was my fault.

The city threw a ticker-tape bon voyage for the boys of Precinct 5-0. It was really inspiring. Elmo and the Harlots roasted weenies on a funeral pyre.

Lucifers Crank came and went, then went to Bangladesh to kick helium. Faust took Hollywood by storm in *The Mickey Rooney Story*, and Pederast turned the Mars Bar into a home for unwed mothers.

Somewhat like a virgin, the Red Planet hangs in the daytime sky, invisible to the naked eye. The EQ got his new marching orders. Training crossing guards for the Indy 500.

And somewhere in outer space Natasha Romilar finally did stand trial by a jury of her peers. Lizzie Borden spat out the verdict with Ghengis Khan looking up her dress — Not Guilty by Reason of Heredity.

And the Korps played on.

As for me, I've got a pentagram in one hand and a yo-yo in the other. See, this galaxy's a gamble, this galaxy's a trip...

## about the author

Blag Dahlia lives in San Francisco where he still looks good in tight pants.

## about the artist

Marc Rude lives in Los Angeles because Hell is for children.

## acknowledgements

The author would like to thank
Liz Belile and Gary Hustwit.
Thank you to the Firesign Theater
and Chris Wetzel.
Special thanks to
the Cafaro family and
Greedy Worldwide.

The artist would like to dedicate this book to the
memory of his sister, Wendy. Special thanks to
Lyn Todd for putting up with his shit.

"Reading *Armed To The Teeth With Lipstick* is something akin to being assaulted with bad puns in the shape of a truncheon."

    **NORMAN MAILER**

"...call it *Finnegan's Colostomy*..."

    **GORE VIDAL**

"As Abelard needed Heloise, as Poe craved his sweet Lenore, so too do Dahlia and Rude need to be silenced— forevermore."

    **STEPHEN HAWKINGS KING**

"Like an infected piercing on an aboriginal dingus, (*Armed To The Teeth With Lipstick* is) both modern and primitive in all the wrong places."

    **CARLOS CASTENEDA**

"(*Armed To The Teeth With Lipstick*) turned an otherwise damp nether region into a vast, parched Sahara..."

    **ANAIS NIN**

"The First Amendment is a sticky mistress. Every once in a while a book like this one comes around. If you're not careful, you just might catch something."

    **STUDS TURKEL**

"Excuse me for shooting my mouth off..."

    **ERNEST HEMINGWAY**

# PARTIAL TEXT of the joint report by NASA and the AMERICAN HEART ASSOCIATION concerning selected passages from the illustrated novel "ARMED to the TEETH with LIPSTICK" and the increased incidence of CORONARY HEMORRHAGE in humans

We, the undersigned, are still confused at this time as to the precise nature of this literary work; whose authors, while presenting themselves psuedonomously, continue to evince a wanton disregard for basic sentence structure, linear narrative, computer generated art and general publishing etiquette. Still, we feel it our duty to inform the book buying public that it faces a danger from within every bit as embarrassing and potentially explosive as angina or hardening of the atmosphere in collusion with forces well beyond the control of modern man or his ape-like ancestors, to boldly go where no man, woman or freshly washed child has gone before in securing a possible cure for the common crab nebula and hence the very meaning of death itself.
Four score and seven years ago deep space was as cold and distant as a Calvinist toilet brush, now we skip to my lou with the forces of evil and just let the chips fall where they may. But, there is a ray of light shining like a soupcon of semen where all around is darkness. That force, if you will, is called good old fashined horse sense, a commodity sorely lacking in today's poncified moral demeanor.
Time was we respected the cop on his beat with a club and the scent of fresh lilacs and booty was something to come home to, not to be sneezed at. Times have changed. We know now that you can't subsist on plantains even if we wanted to. And some of us want to. Myocardial infarction strikes nine out of ten astronomers, and this is the amazing part, past the age of reason, 1994 AD. Meanwhile, deep space gets deeper with no visible end in sight. I don't know about you, but I've gotta be me, so to speak.
Books like this don't help us. They don't enlighten us, or point us toward a better tomorrow. What they do is cause heart attacks and super novas. They work their way into the fiber of our space program and strangle it to death from above. And just when you think it might be over, there's a new predator waiting in the wings.
Bad puns and dodgy bohemian ethics may fly in San Francisco, fat boy, but who died and made you king of the airport newsrack? Ever stop to think there's a time and a place, you just ain't invited? A great man once said, "don't be sharp, don't be flat, just be natural." And we all need a hearse for our good intentions.
The sections to be avoided at all costs: when Doolan gets all fukked up; when Doolan gets confused; when Doolan shoots someone; when Natasha gets randy; When Randy Gets Randy (sorry, that was my first film); after the intercourse barn; right before and during the intercourse barn; three coins in the intercourse barn; Sir Thomas Hardy; and several not worth mentioning except in passing.
When I was matriculating at Vasser I always tried to keep my fly out in the open so people could get with my hang-ups. I'm better now, but are we? And how far have we come to a literary canon that we can feel good about, that we can tell our children of in hushed whispers and sit around the campfire correcting gerund phrases and times when 'Y' is a vowel and stuff. No more can we sit idly by while phrases are mangled and foreigners run free like limpid mules, cursing the Statue of Liberty and playing Hamlet to the Planet of the Apes.
Arise you stinking lizard queens, you've got nothing to shit but the hypes.
Hard corollaries abound: the hour is near, but is anybody happy?
It's been said that an ocean of fish can produce a basket of plutonium. If they can put a man on the moon, why can't I be bothered anymore? Because them's the breaks, kid. One day you're sitting in the wings, the next day you're wearing them. God is good, but he's busy and he forgets things. That's why I need an agent. Blessed is he who comes if you catch my meaning and I'm sure that if you don't you can at least act like you know.
And so I'm offering this simple phrase, for folks from five to channel two, though it's been said, first by guys then by gays, the American Space Program is not now nor has it ever been a haven for pissants, derelicts or anyone from San Diego, and let me elaborate on this further, it's forty-five miles to Satanville, but only thirty-five light years away. El Cajon can be annexed to Mexico in a swap and we retain all them purty senoritas, what do you say, Chico, is it a deal? Did that flap on the beef curtains tweek you up proper-like?
It's three groins in the fountain, no hits no errors and an action Jackson scenario of doom and mass hysteria. Boo Radley leaks pustules and chloroform sunshines on peonies too lusty and spangled to be real. On dasher, dancer, and the whole McVixen Crew I'd like to take this opportunity to thank all of you little people who helped to make this piece a reality, first of all my aunts, uncles, cousins, second cousins, second cousins once removed and everyone at the Department of Motor Vehicles. You folks are the shiznit, really.
Come hello highwater your poor, your mangled, your grotesque masses yearning to breathe free, as free as the ass knows, like heaven and hormones. Try getting to Pittsburgh with one shoe or inflating the jaws of life for a guy you don't even know already. Venus is crowded with speckled herpetica, most arachnids bleed mucosa and salvage the plantains, always the plantains. Bryan and Bryce lurched hard for the angry member, as Ramon teased them at arms length with a piece of twine and an androids naughty girl necrostic five nights out of five for a McGarrett sized feast of corn cob souffle, hard targets and nine pound Hillary giblets. Place peniles in utera rosary NASCAR plague with a capital crimean whore lot or fuel for the fur lords and rubber barons, the bees knees and the ejectors, the terpsichore, hell harlot, the bob goblin of never been, never was, never Marcus Wilby, so help me God.
The Verdict- We the people find the aforementioned "book" to be a real piece of fukking shit and label it too shocking for human consumption.

Thank you for your consideration.

# NASA and the AMERICAN HEART ASSOCIATION